STONE ARCH BOOKS
a capstone imprint

THE BATMAN STRIKES!®

STONE ARCH BOOKS™

Published in 2015 by Stone Arch Books
A Capstone Imprint
1710 Roe Crest Drive
North Mankato, MN 56003
www.capstonepub.com

Originally published by DC Comics in the U.S. in single magazine form as The Batman Strikes! #10.

DC Comics
1700 Broadway, New York, NY 10019
A Warner Bros. Entertainment Company

Printed in China by Nordica.
0914/CA21401510
092014 008470NORDS15

Cataloging-in-Publication Data is available at the Library of Congress website.
ISBN: 978-1-4342-9655-9 (library binding)

Summary: Three college students find themselves trapped by the vicious Man-Bat. When the power goes out in the asylum, Batman is there to take on his evil foe.

STONE ARCH BOOKS
Ashley C. Andersen Zantop *Publisher*
Michael Dahl *Editorial Director*
Eliza Leahy *Editor*
Heather Kindseth *Creative Director*
Peggie Carley *Designer*
Tori Abraham *Production Specialist*

DC COMICS
Nachie Castro *Original U.S. Editor*

MAN-BAT'S SNEAK ATTACK!

BILL MATHENY ....WRITER
CHRISTOPHER JONES ....PENCILLER
TERRY BEATTY...INKER
HEROIC AGE..COLORIST
PHIL BALSMAN ....LETTERER

BATMAN CREATED BY
BOB KANE

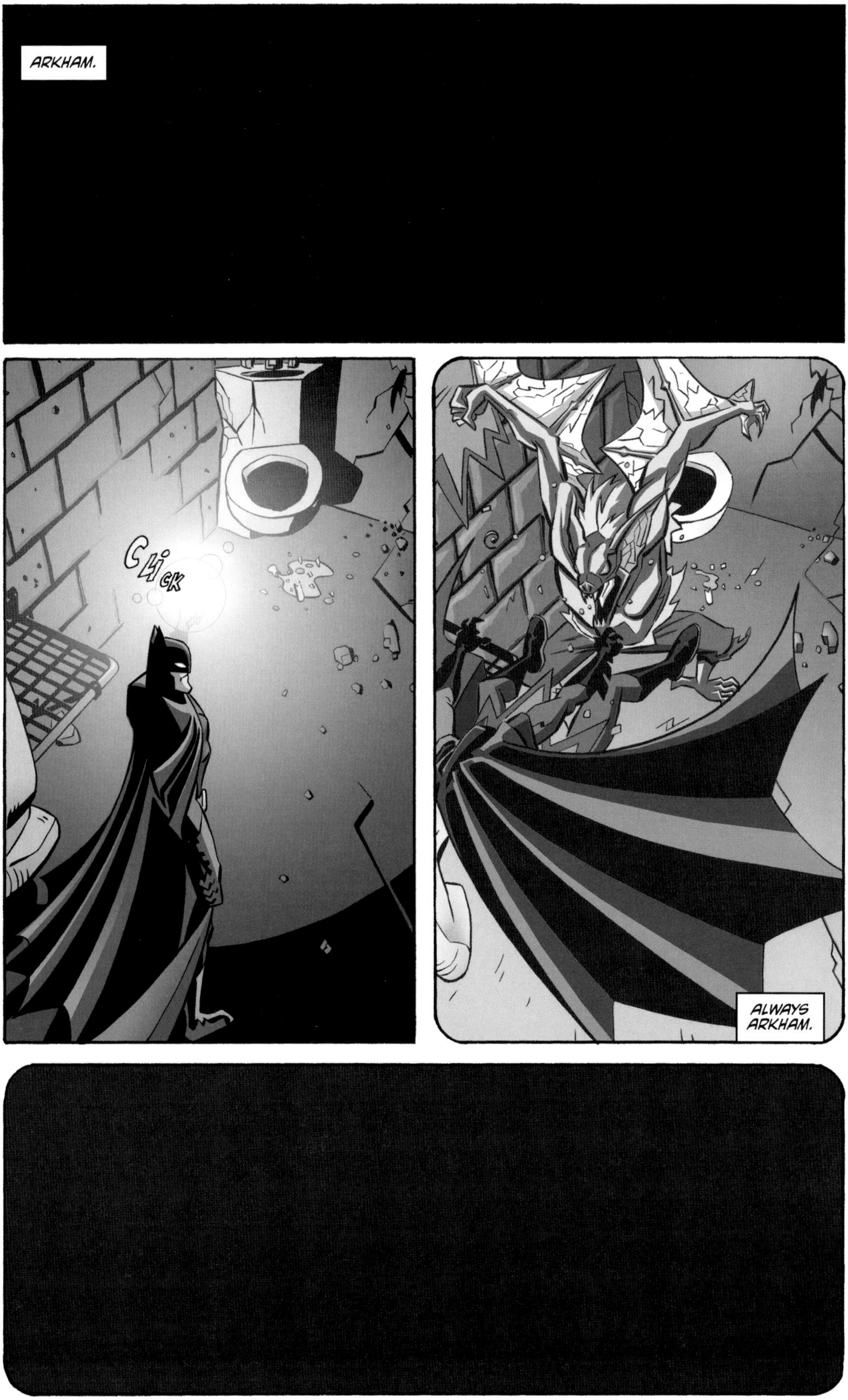
ARKHAM.
CLICK
ALWAYS ARKHAM.

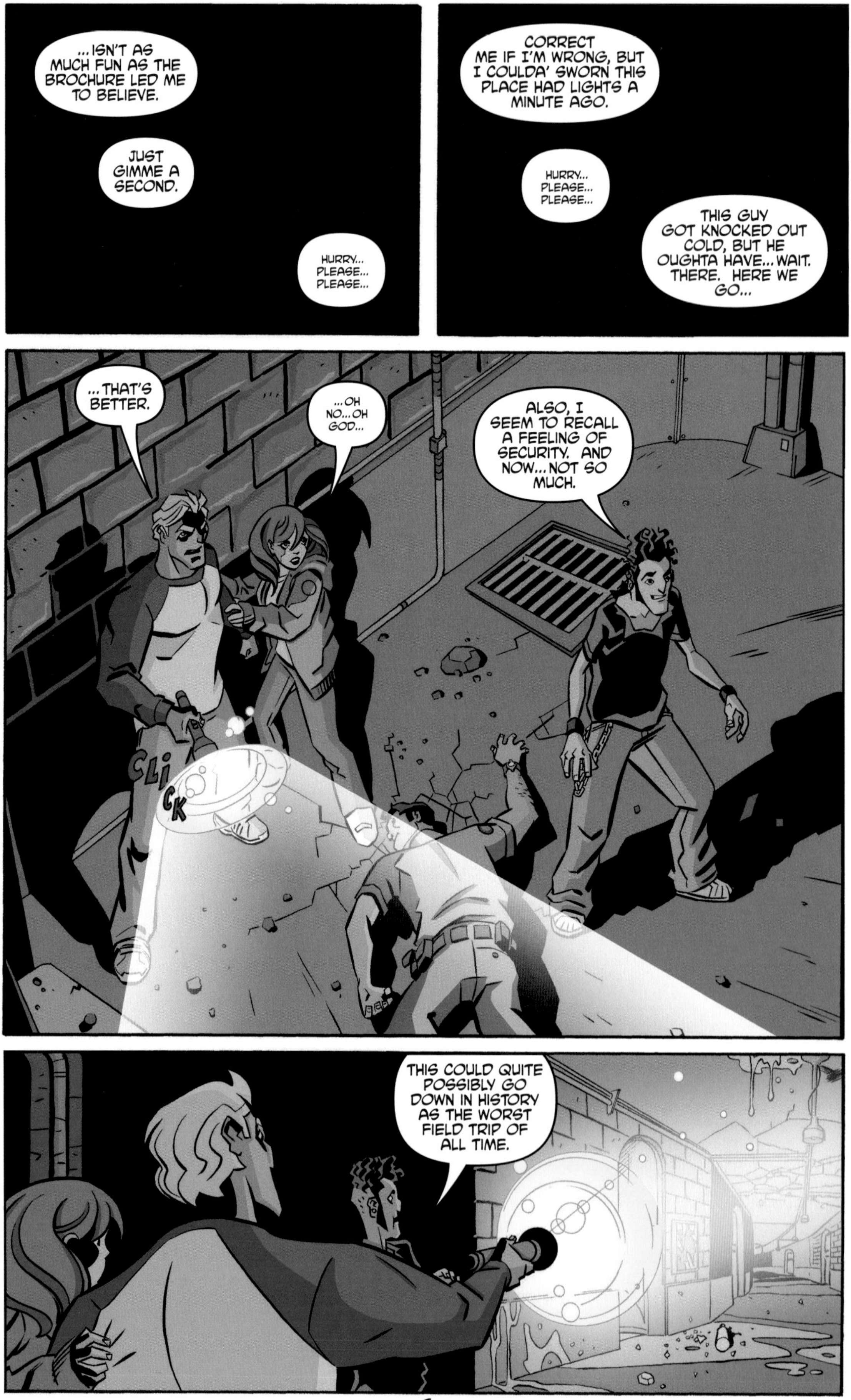
...ISN'T AS MUCH FUN AS THE BROCHURE LED ME TO BELIEVE.
JUST GIMME A SECOND.
HURRY... PLEASE... PLEASE...
CORRECT ME IF I'M WRONG, BUT I COULDA' SWORN THIS PLACE HAD LIGHTS A MINUTE AGO.
HURRY... PLEASE... PLEASE...
THIS GUY GOT KNOCKED OUT COLD, BUT HE OUGHTA HAVE... WAIT. THERE. HERE WE GO...
...THAT'S BETTER.
...OH NO...OH GOD...
ALSO, I SEEM TO RECALL A FEELING OF SECURITY. AND NOW...NOT SO MUCH.
CLICK
THIS COULD QUITE POSSIBLY GO DOWN IN HISTORY AS THE WORST FIELD TRIP OF ALL TIME.

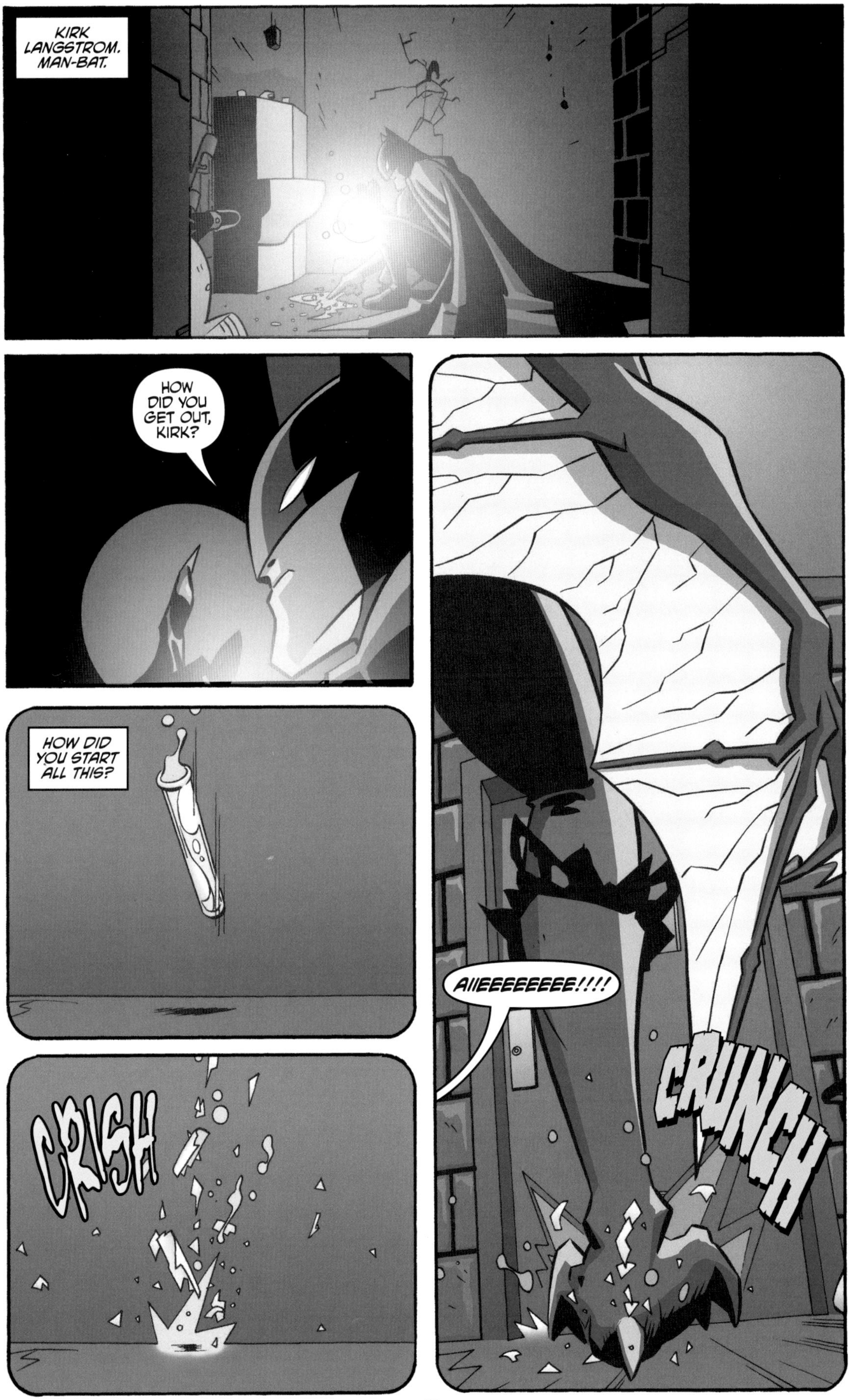
KIRK LANGSTROM. MAN-BAT.
HOW DID YOU GET OUT, KIRK?
HOW DID YOU START ALL THIS?
CRISH
AIIEEEEEEEEE!!!!
CRUNCH

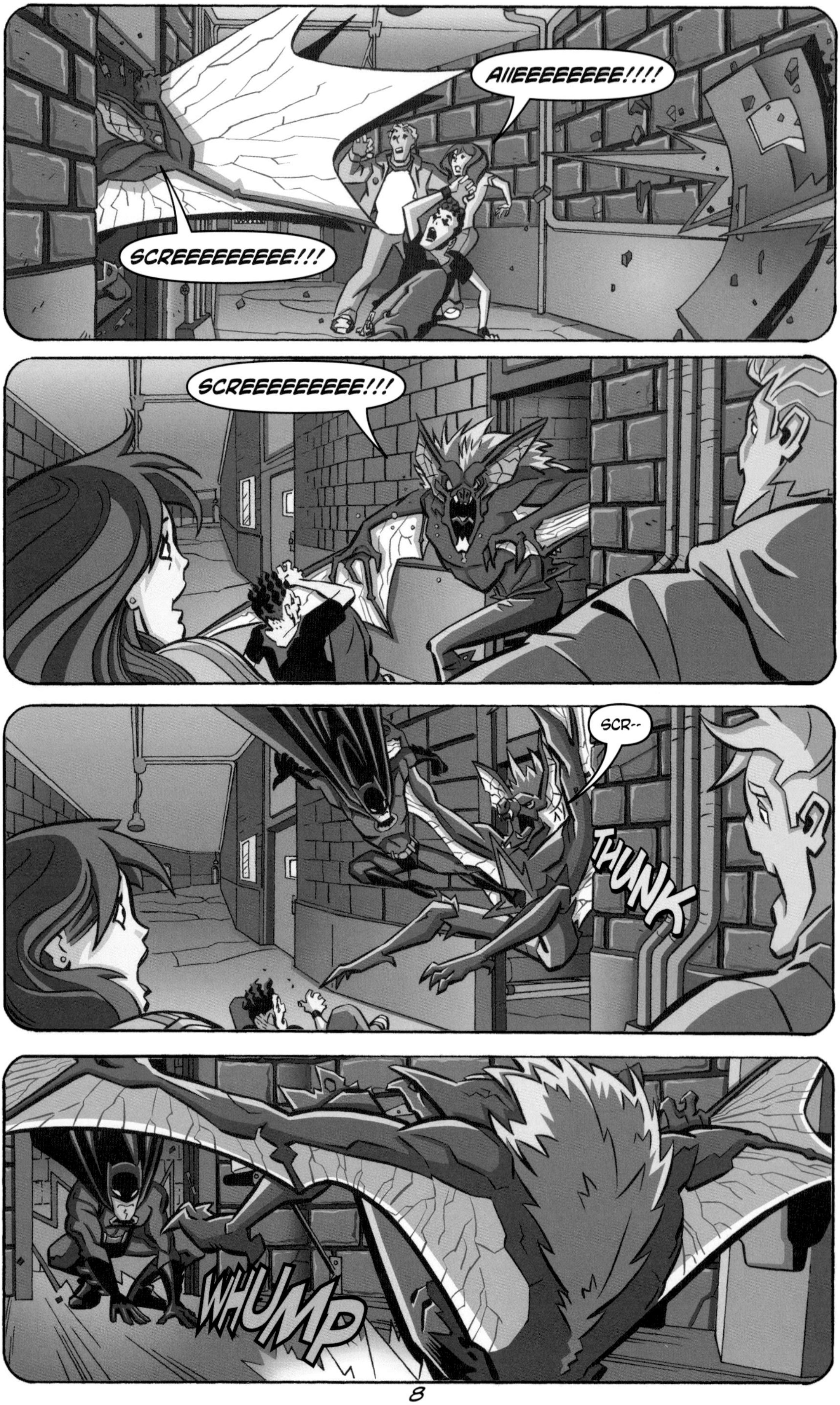
AIIEEEEEEEEE!!!!
SCREEEEEEEEEE!!!
SCREEEEEEEEEE!!!
SCR--
THUNK
WHUMP

WHUMP

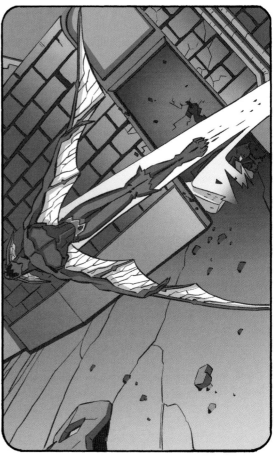

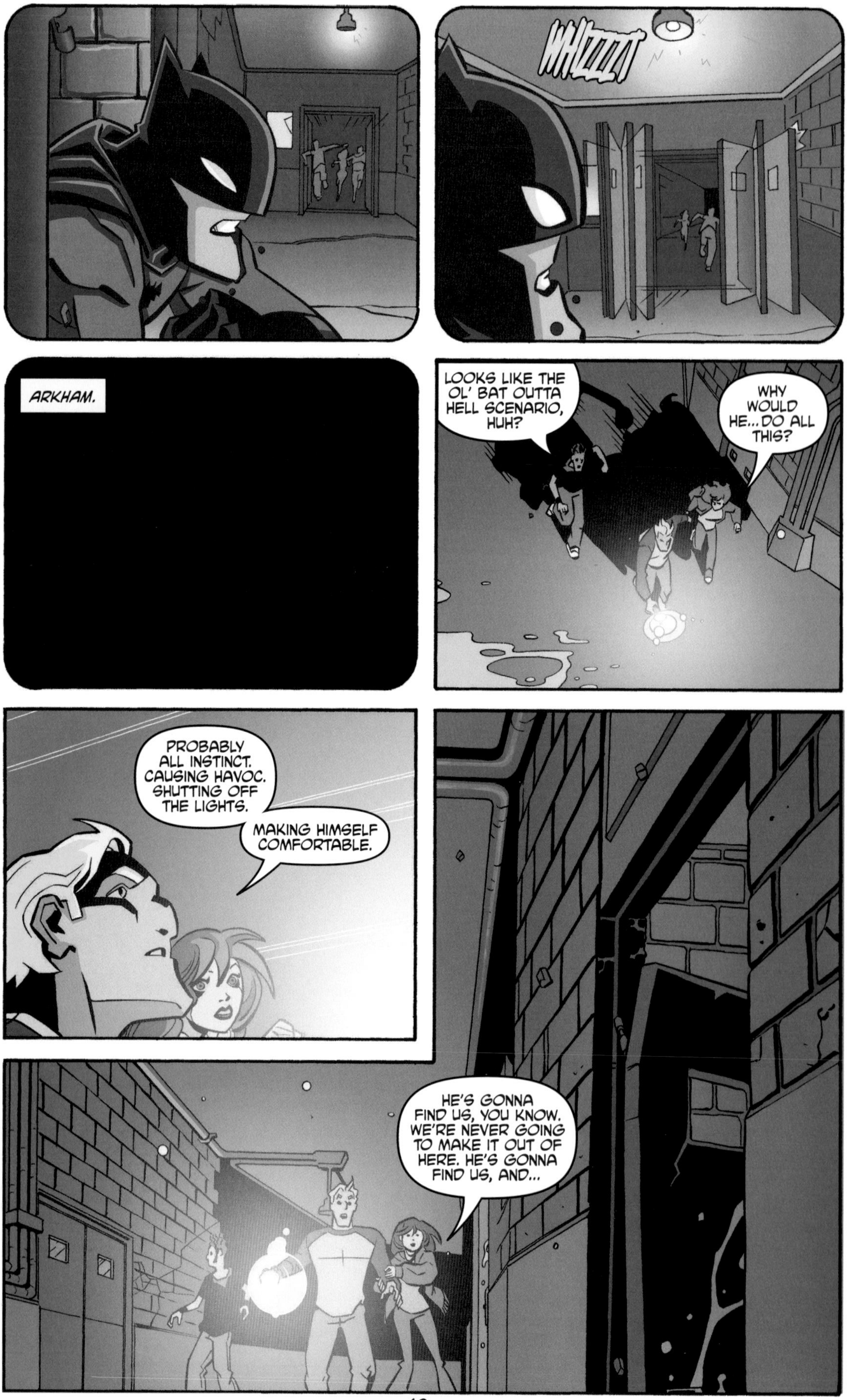
WHIZZZZT
ARKHAM.
LOOKS LIKE THE OL' BAT OUTTA HELL SCENARIO, HUH?
WHY WOULD HE...DO ALL THIS?
PROBABLY ALL INSTINCT. CAUSING HAVOC. SHUTTING OFF THE LIGHTS.
MAKING HIMSELF COMFORTABLE.
HE'S GONNA FIND US, YOU KNOW. WE'RE NEVER GOING TO MAKE IT OUT OF HERE. HE'S GONNA FIND US, AND...

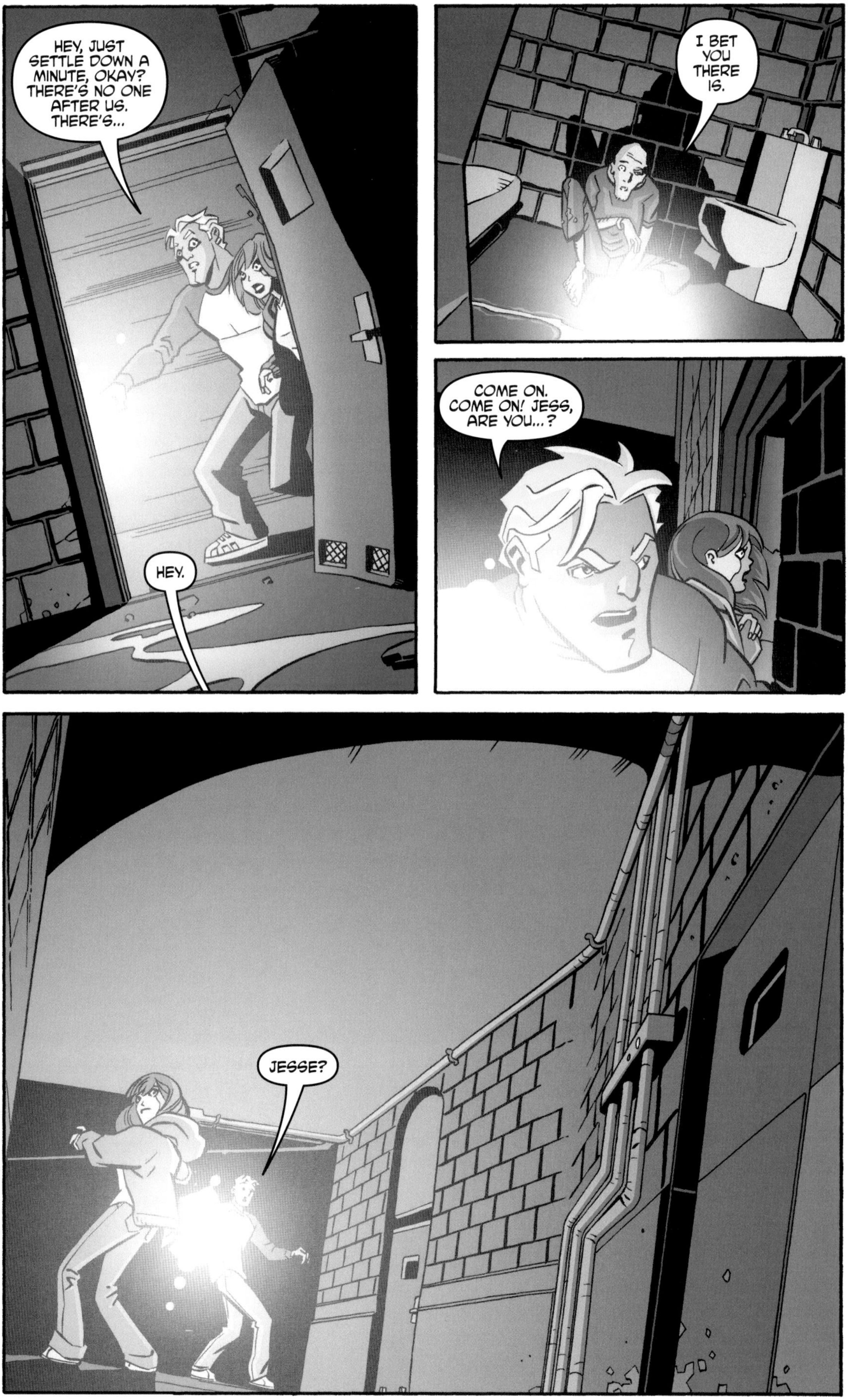
HEY, JUST SETTLE DOWN A MINUTE, OKAY? THERE'S NO ONE AFTER US. THERE'S...
HEY.
I BET YOU THERE IS.
COME ON. COME ON! JESS, ARE YOU...?
JESSE?

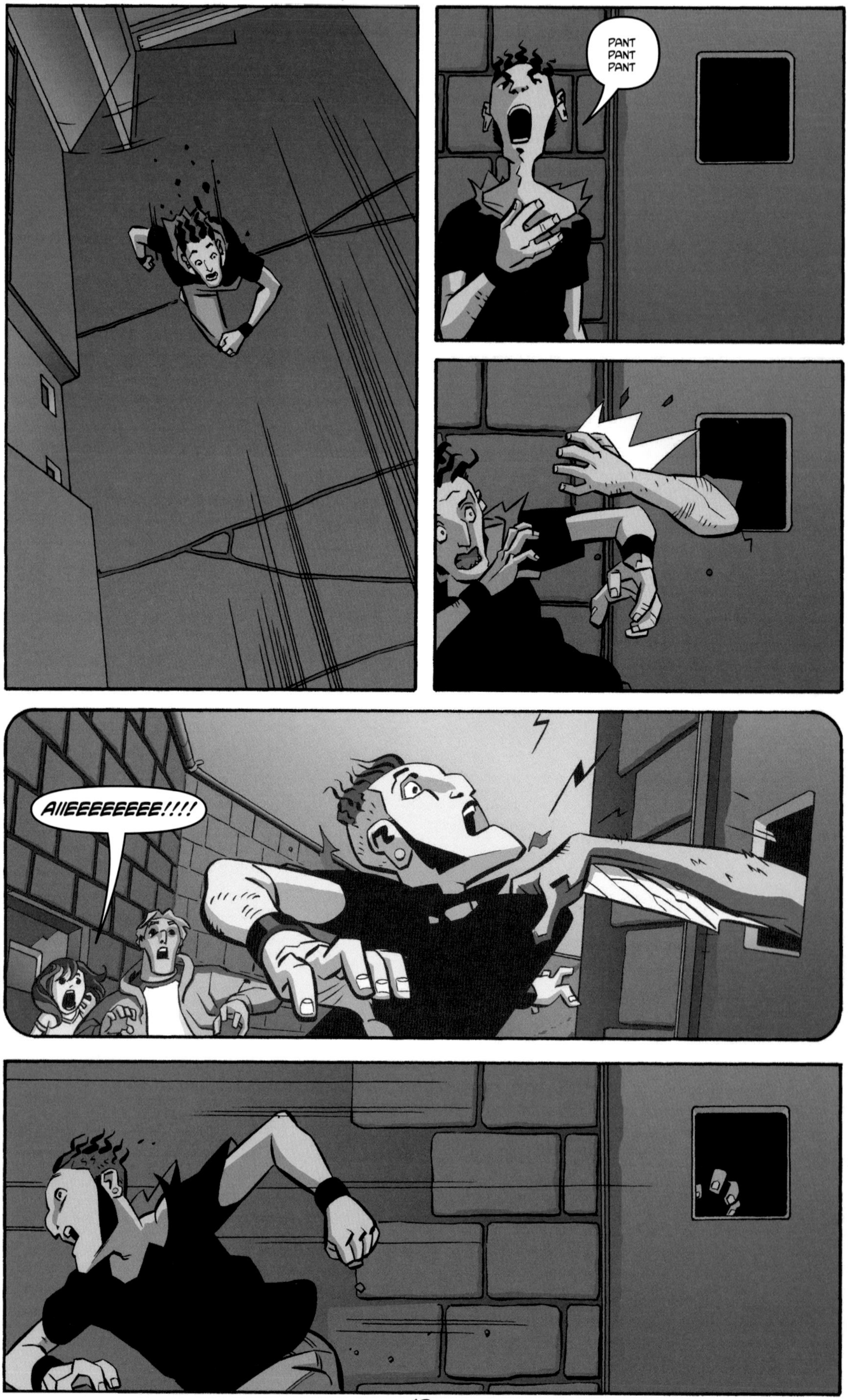
PANT
PANT
PANT
AIIEEEEEEEE!!!!

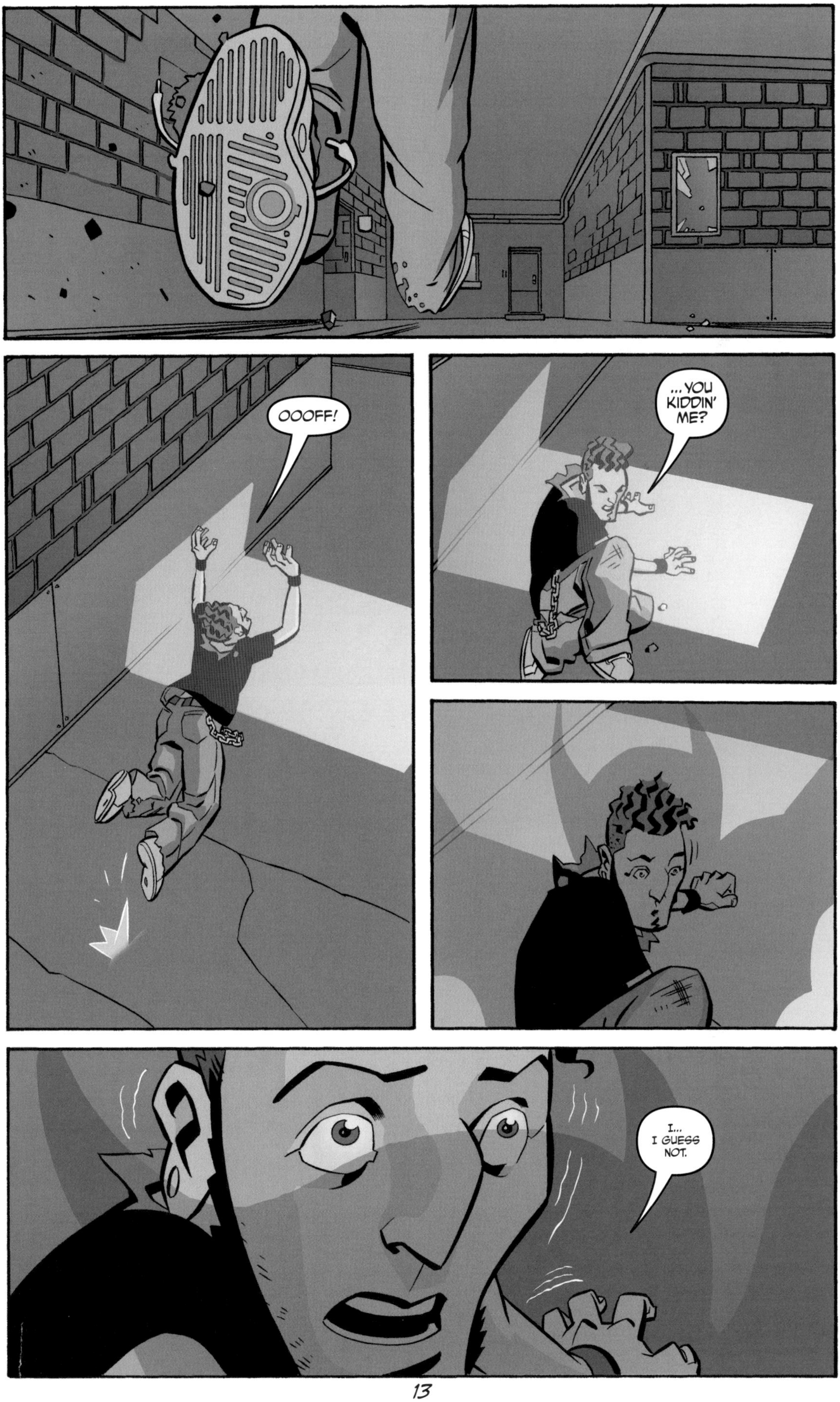
OOOFF!
...YOU KIDDIN' ME?
I... I GUESS NOT.

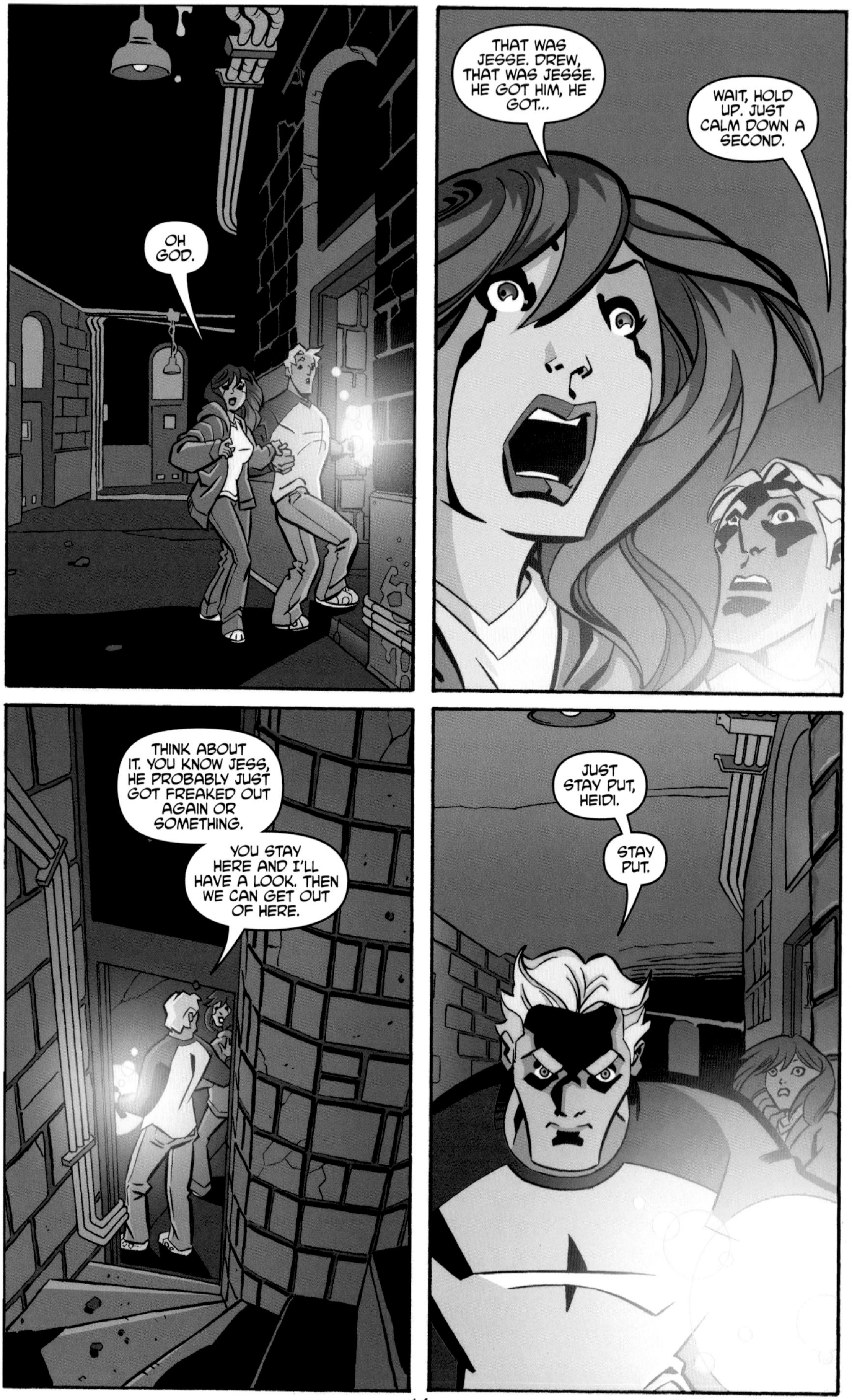
OH GOD.
THAT WAS JESSE. DREW, THAT WAS JESSE. HE GOT HIM, HE GOT...
WAIT, HOLD UP. JUST CALM DOWN A SECOND.
THINK ABOUT IT. YOU KNOW JESS, HE PROBABLY JUST GOT FREAKED OUT AGAIN OR SOMETHING.
YOU STAY HERE AND I'LL HAVE A LOOK. THEN WE CAN GET OUT OF HERE.
JUST STAY PUT, HEIDI.
STAY PUT.

OKAY, WELL, THIS ROOM LOOKS FAMILIAR...
"...UNFORTUNATELY."
...OUR RECREATION ROOM WHERE OUR PATIENTS HAVE A CHANCE TO INTERACT WITH ONE ANOTHER, BUILDING BACK VALUABLE SOCIAL SKILLS.
AND WHAT'S DOWN THAT WAY, DOCTOR?
OH, I DON'T THINK YOUR PSYCHOLOGY PROFESSOR WOULD APPRECIATE MY TAKING YOU KIDS DOWN THAT HALL. NO, THAT WAY'S OFF LIMITS TO TOUR GROUPS. THAT'S THE WING OF THE ASYLUM WHERE WE HOUSE OUR MORE... DIFFICULT INMATES.
NOW IF YOU'LL ALL CONTINUE THIS WAY, WE'RE COMING UP TO OUR GROUP THERAPY ROOM, AND IF WE'RE LUCKY, WE MIGHT JUST BE IN TIME FOR THE SIX O'CLOCK SESSION...
WELL, THAT SOUNDED LIKE A CHALLENGE TO ME. YOU GUYS ARE STILL GAME, RIGHT?

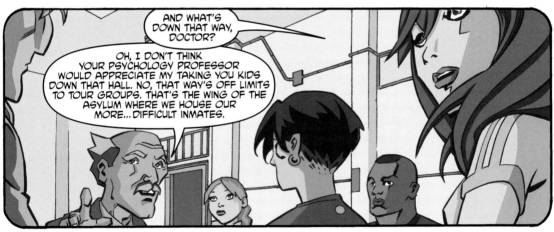

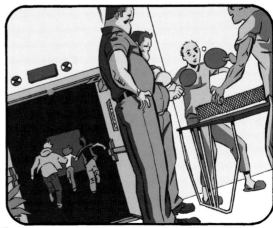

WH!R WH!R WH!R

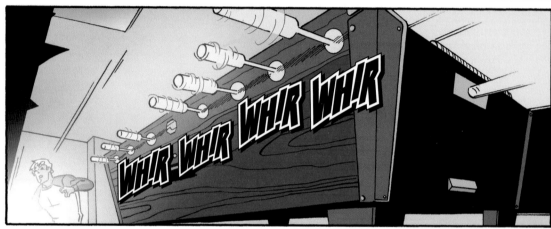

WH!R WH!R WH!R WH!R

FLAP RUSTLE FLAP

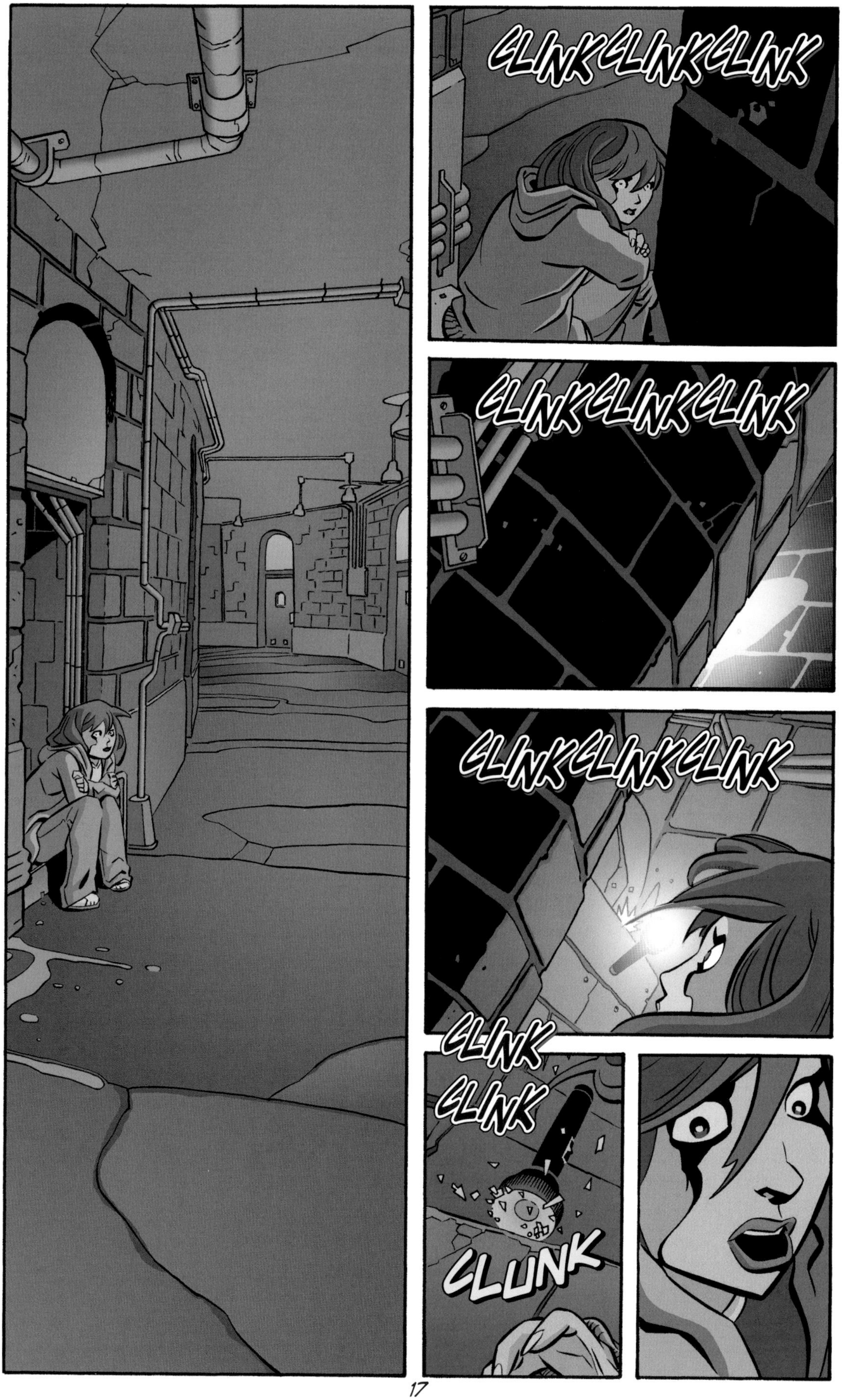
CLINKCLINKCLINK
CLINKCLINKCLINK
CLINKCLINKCLINK
CLINK
CLINK
CLUNK

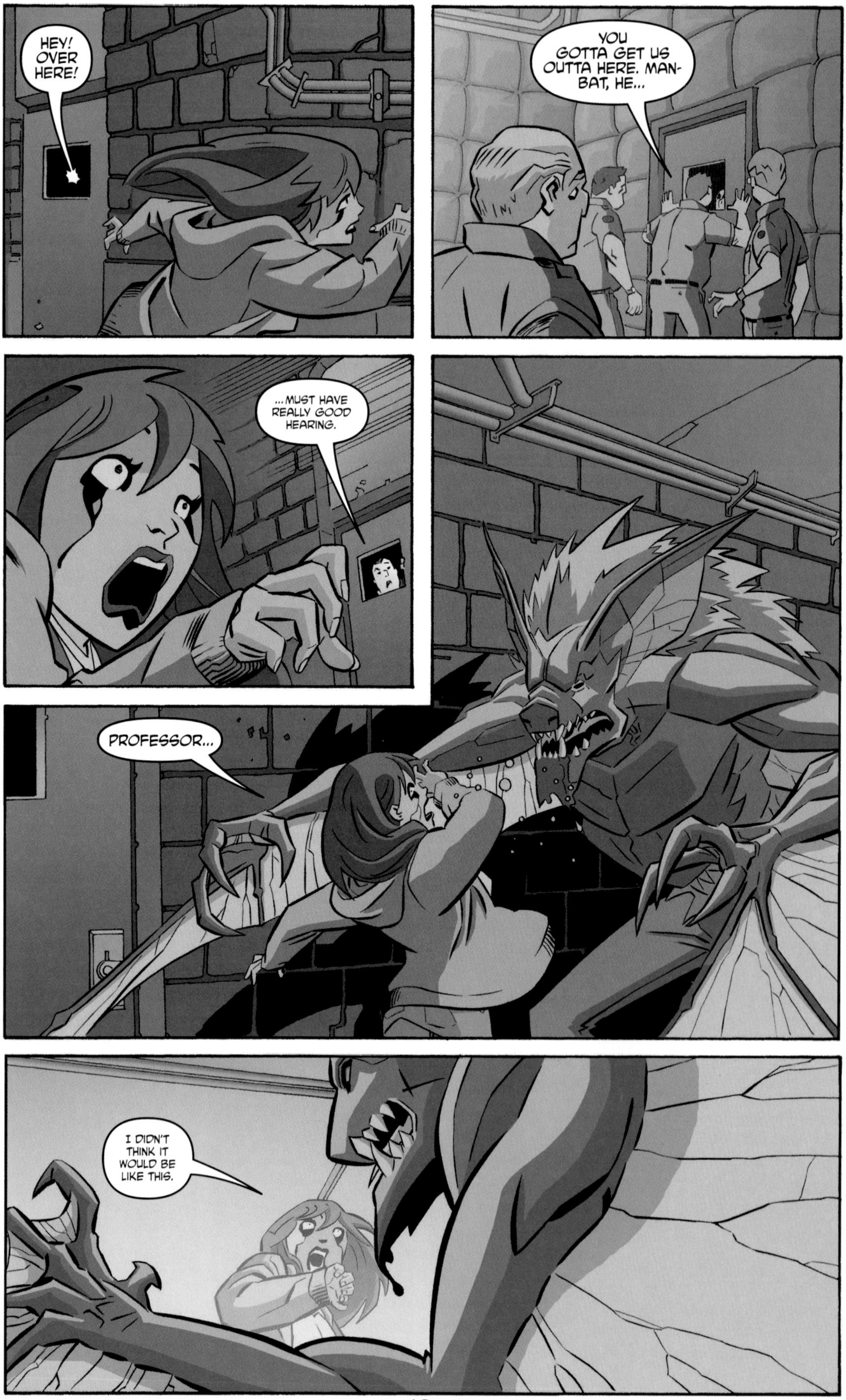
HEY! OVER HERE!
YOU GOTTA GET US OUTTA HERE. MAN-BAT, HE...
...MUST HAVE REALLY GOOD HEARING.
PROFESSOR...
I DIDN'T THINK IT WOULD BE LIKE THIS.

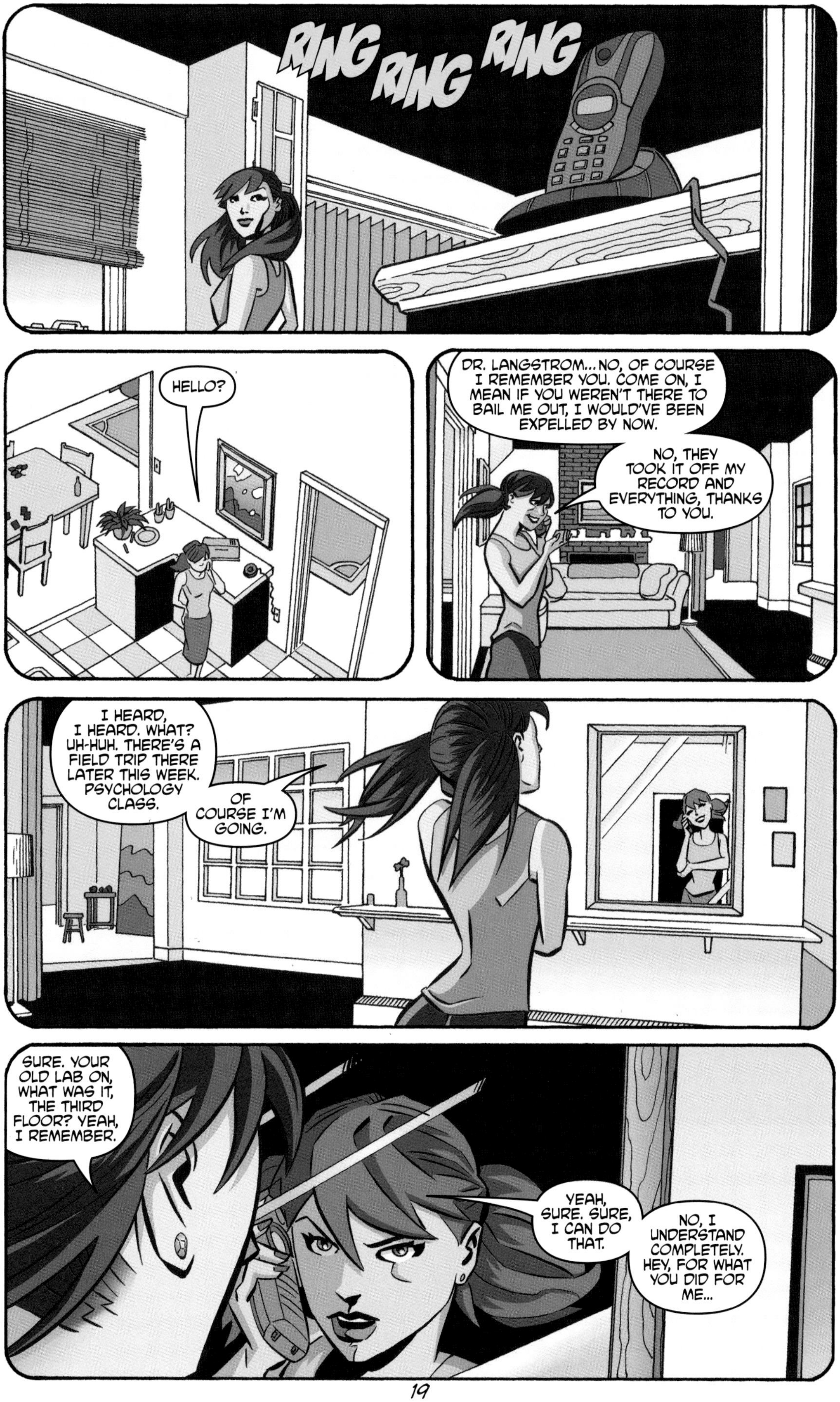
RING RING RING
HELLO?
DR. LANGSTROM...NO, OF COURSE I REMEMBER YOU. COME ON, I MEAN IF YOU WEREN'T THERE TO BAIL ME OUT, I WOULD'VE BEEN EXPELLED BY NOW.
NO, THEY TOOK IT OFF MY RECORD AND EVERYTHING, THANKS TO YOU.
I HEARD, I HEARD. WHAT? UH-HUH. THERE'S A FIELD TRIP THERE LATER THIS WEEK. PSYCHOLOGY CLASS.
OF COURSE I'M GOING.
SURE. YOUR OLD LAB ON, WHAT WAS IT, THE THIRD FLOOR? YEAH, I REMEMBER.
YEAH, SURE. SURE, I CAN DO THAT.
NO, I UNDERSTAND COMPLETELY. HEY, FOR WHAT YOU DID FOR ME...

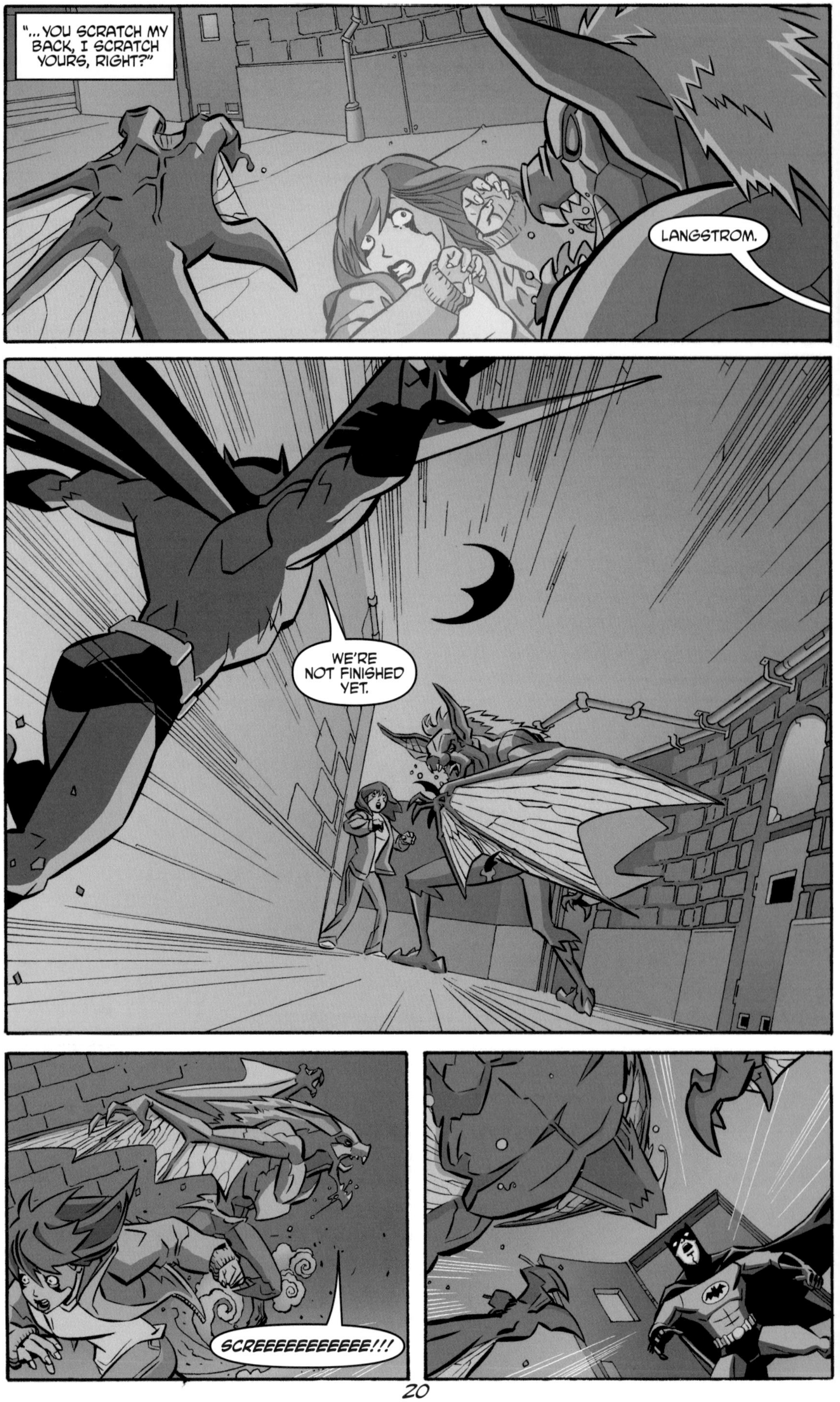
"...YOU SCRATCH MY BACK, I SCRATCH YOURS, RIGHT?"
LANGSTROM.
WE'RE NOT FINISHED YET.
SCREEEEEEEEEEEE!!!

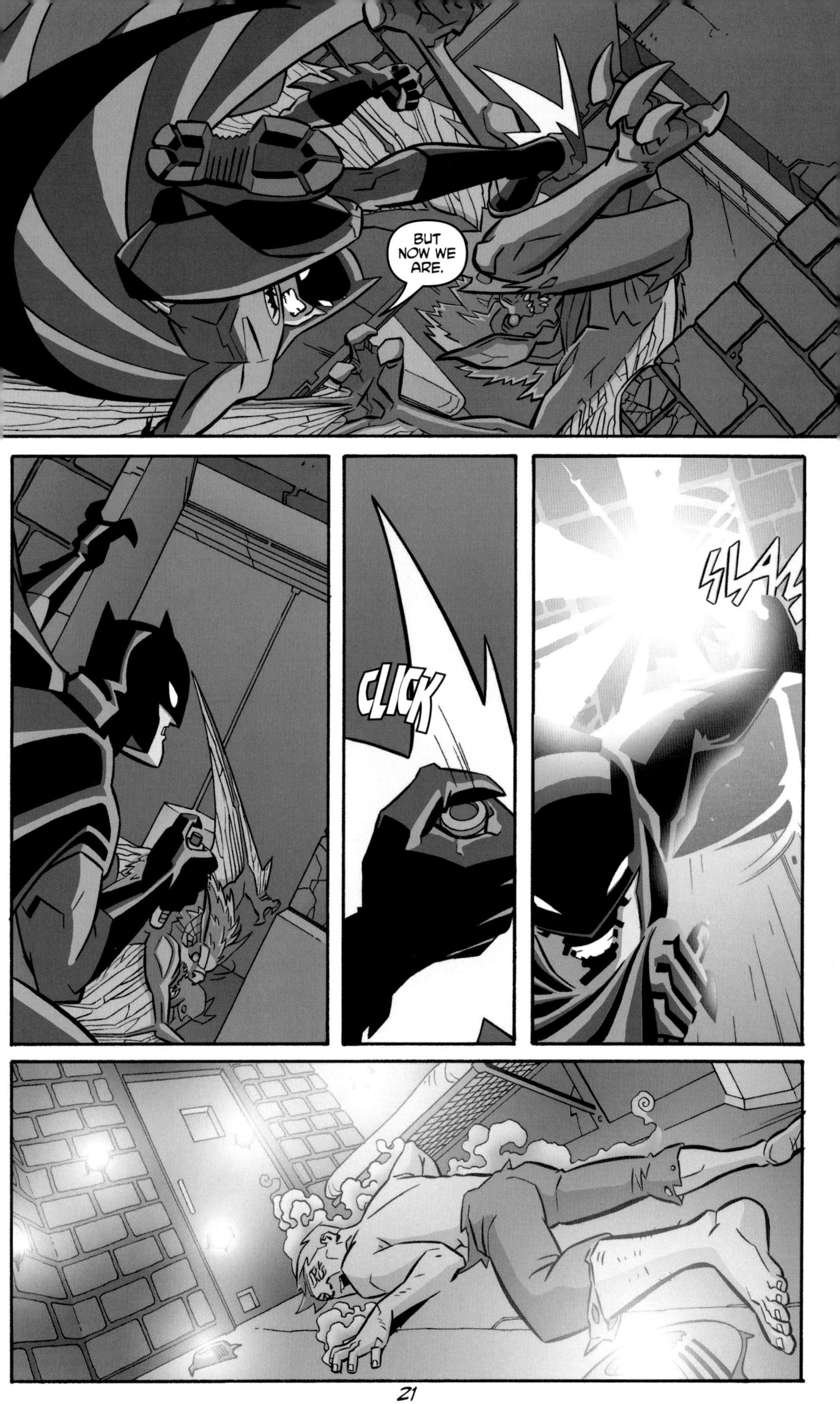
BUT NOW WE ARE.
CLICK
SLAM

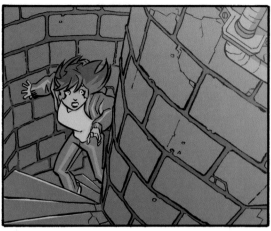

HE SHOULD BE AROUND HERE SOME...

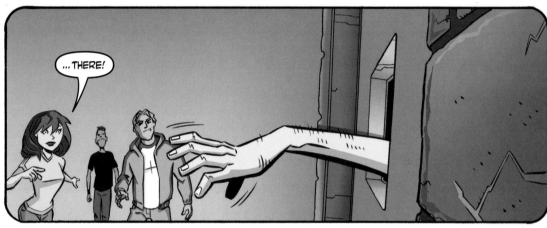

...THERE!

IT WAS RIGHT WHERE YOU TOLD ME IT WOULD BE, DR. LANGSTROM. RIGHT IN THE BACK OF THE CABINET.

GOOD, GOOD. THIS OUGHT TO DO JUST FINE.

WAIT, I THOUGHT YOU SAID... DOCTOR?

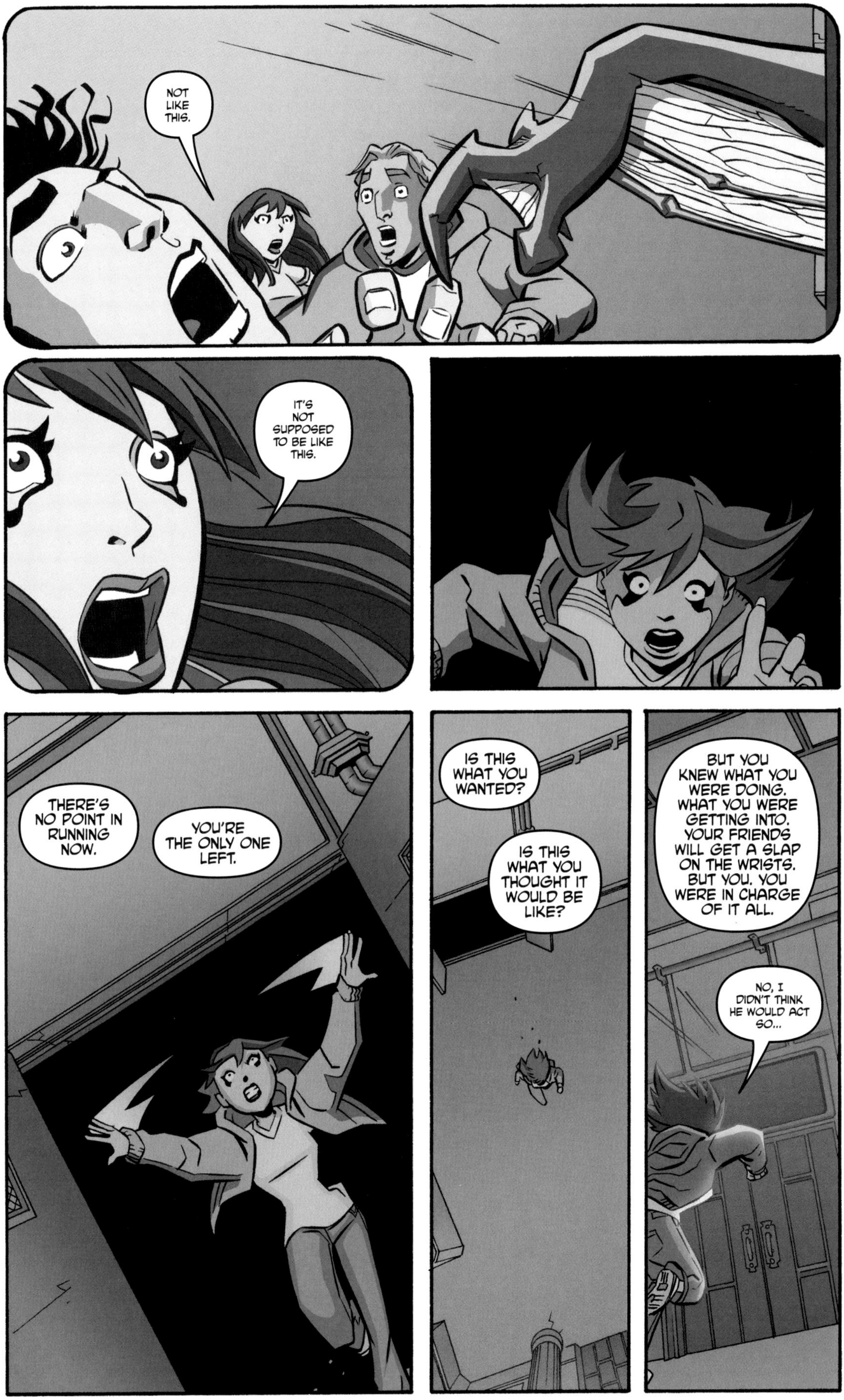
NOT LIKE THIS.
IT'S NOT SUPPOSED TO BE LIKE THIS.
THERE'S NO POINT IN RUNNING NOW.
YOU'RE THE ONLY ONE LEFT.
IS THIS WHAT YOU WANTED?
IS THIS WHAT YOU THOUGHT IT WOULD BE LIKE?
BUT YOU KNEW WHAT YOU WERE DOING. WHAT YOU WERE GETTING INTO. YOUR FRIENDS WILL GET A SLAP ON THE WRISTS. BUT YOU. YOU WERE IN CHARGE OF IT ALL.
NO, I DIDN'T THINK HE WOULD ACT SO...

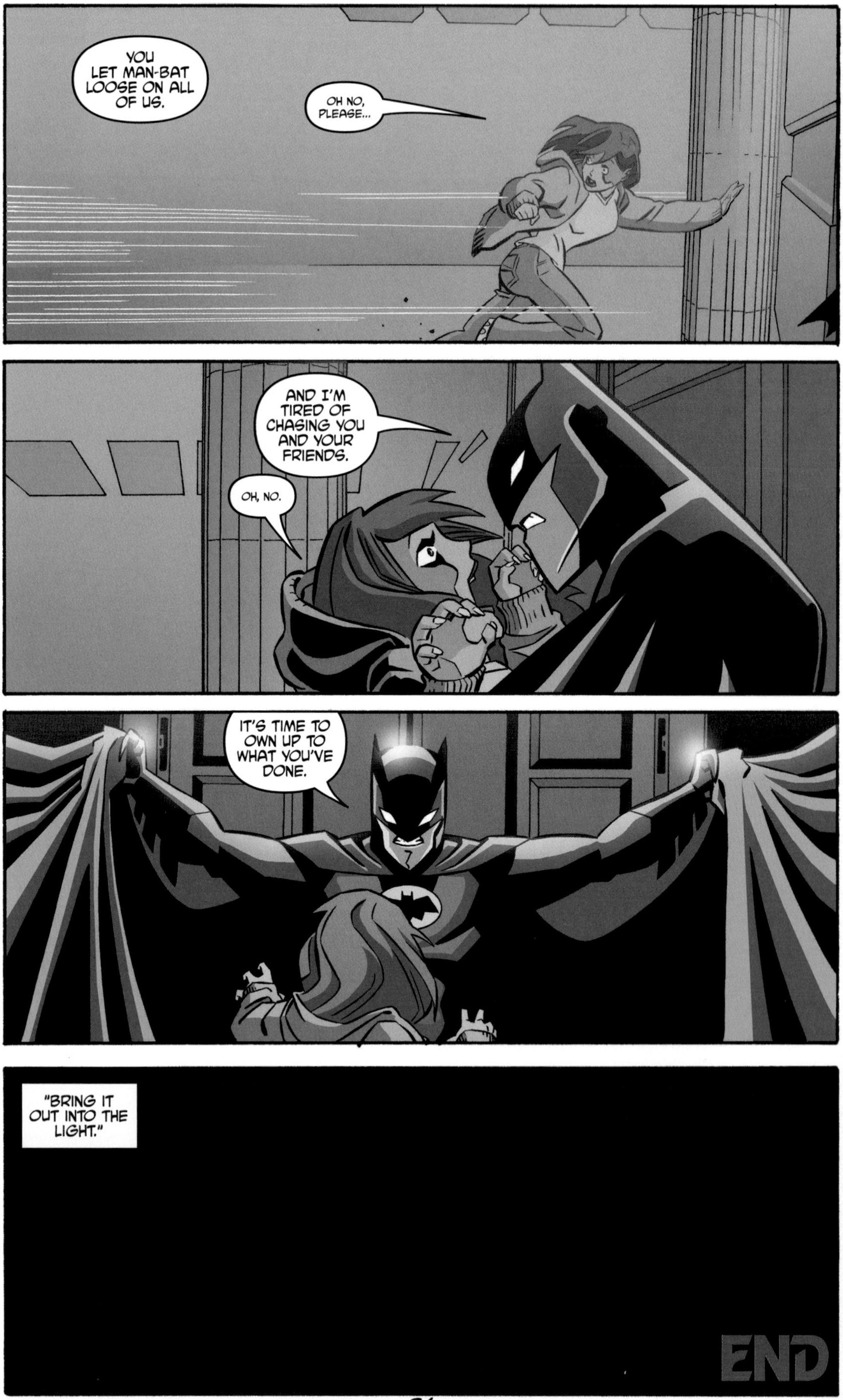
YOU LET MAN-BAT LOOSE ON ALL OF US.
OH NO, PLEASE...
AND I'M TIRED OF CHASING YOU AND YOUR FRIENDS.
OH, NO.
IT'S TIME TO OWN UP TO WHAT YOU'VE DONE.
"BRING IT OUT INTO THE LIGHT."
END

CREATORS

BILL MATHENY WRITER

Along with comics like THE BATMAN STRIKES, Bill Matheny has written for TV series including KRYPTO THE SUPERDOG, WHERE'S WALDO, A PUP NAMED SCOOBY-DOO, and many others.

CHRISTOPHER JONES PENCILLER

Christopher Jones is an artist who has worked for DC Comics, Image, Malibu, Caliber, and Sundragon Comics.

TERRY BEATTY INKER

Terry Beatty has inked THE BATMAN STRIKES! and BATMAN: THE BRAVE AND THE BOLD as well as several other DC Comics graphic novels.

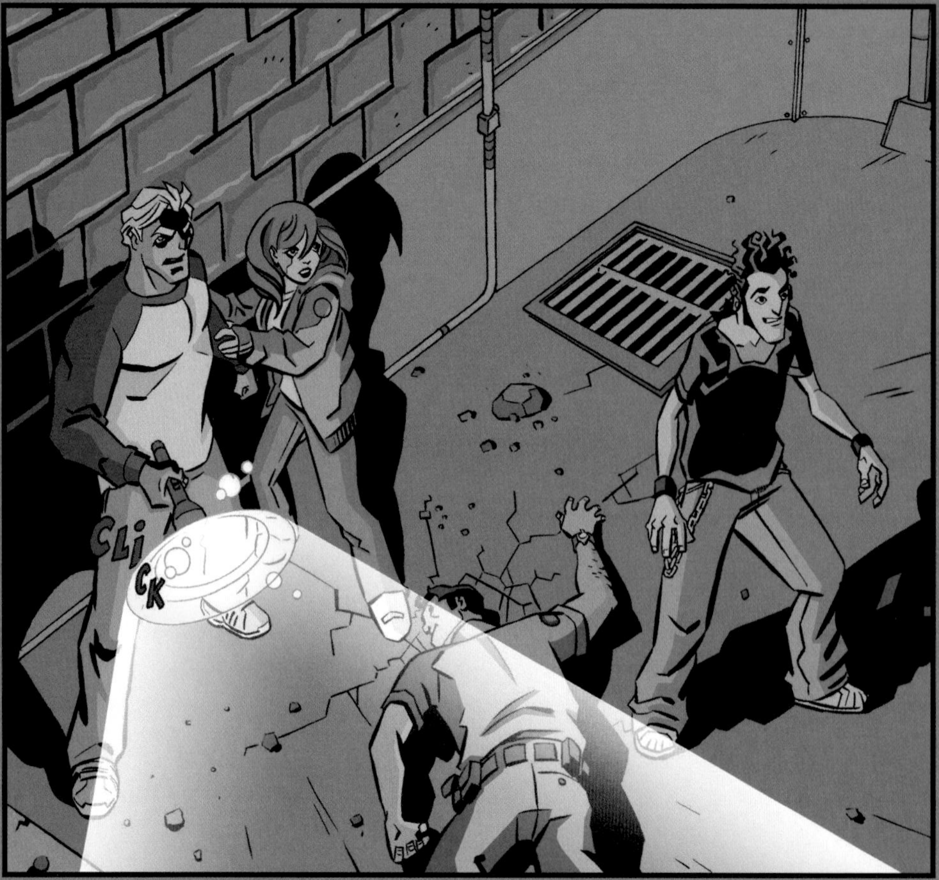
CLICK

GLOSSARY

appreciate (uh-PREE-shee-ayt)--to value somebody or something

asylum (uh-SYE-luhm)--a hospital for people who are mentally ill

brochure (broh-SHOOR)--a booklet that gives information about something

expelled (ik-SPELD)--deprived someone of involvement in school

havoc (HAV-uhk)--great confusion

instinct (IN-stingkt)--knowledge or behavior that comes without thinking

psychology (sye-KAH-luh-jee)--the study of the mind, emotions, and human behavior

scenario (suh-NAYR-ee-oh)--a sequence of events, especially when imagined

therapy (THER-uh-pee)--treatment for an illness, disability, or psychological problem

unfortunately (uhn-FOR-chuh-nit-lee)--unluckily

VISUAL QUESTIONS & PROMPTS

1. Why do you think the artists decided to start the story with a completely black panel?

2. These panels are shaded differently from the others in the story. What kind of feeling does it give those scenes? Why do you think the artists decided to shade them this way?

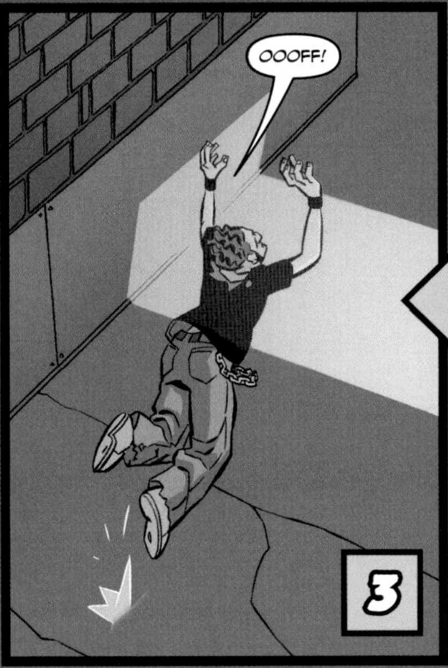
OOOFF!
3

3. How do we know that the boy is tripping in this panel? What gives it away? Is there some other way the artists could have depicted it?

4. How would this scene be different if there was no close-up on Batman's thumb pressing the button?

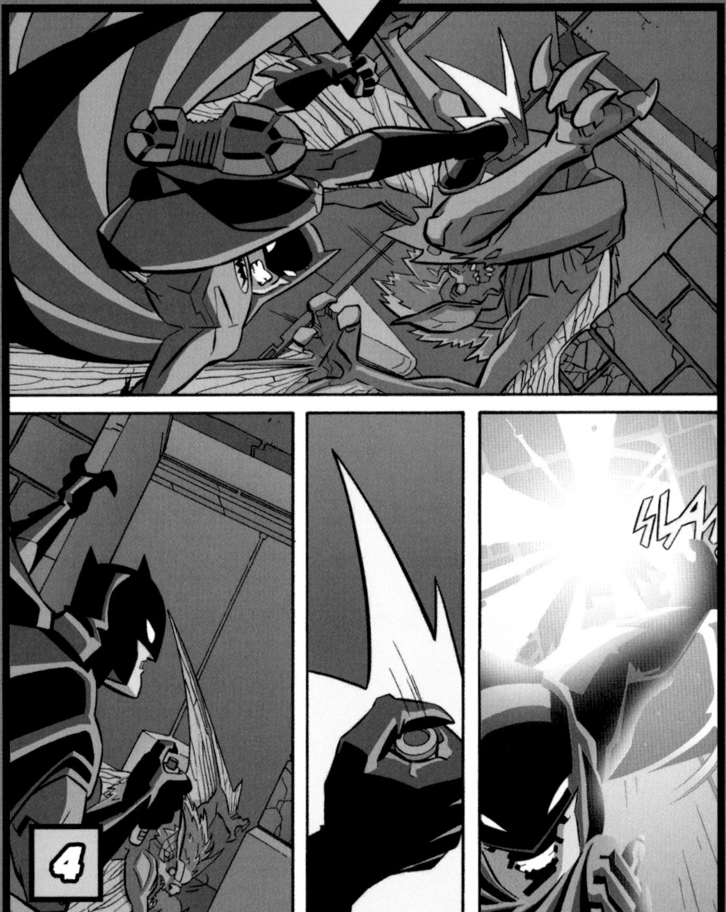
4

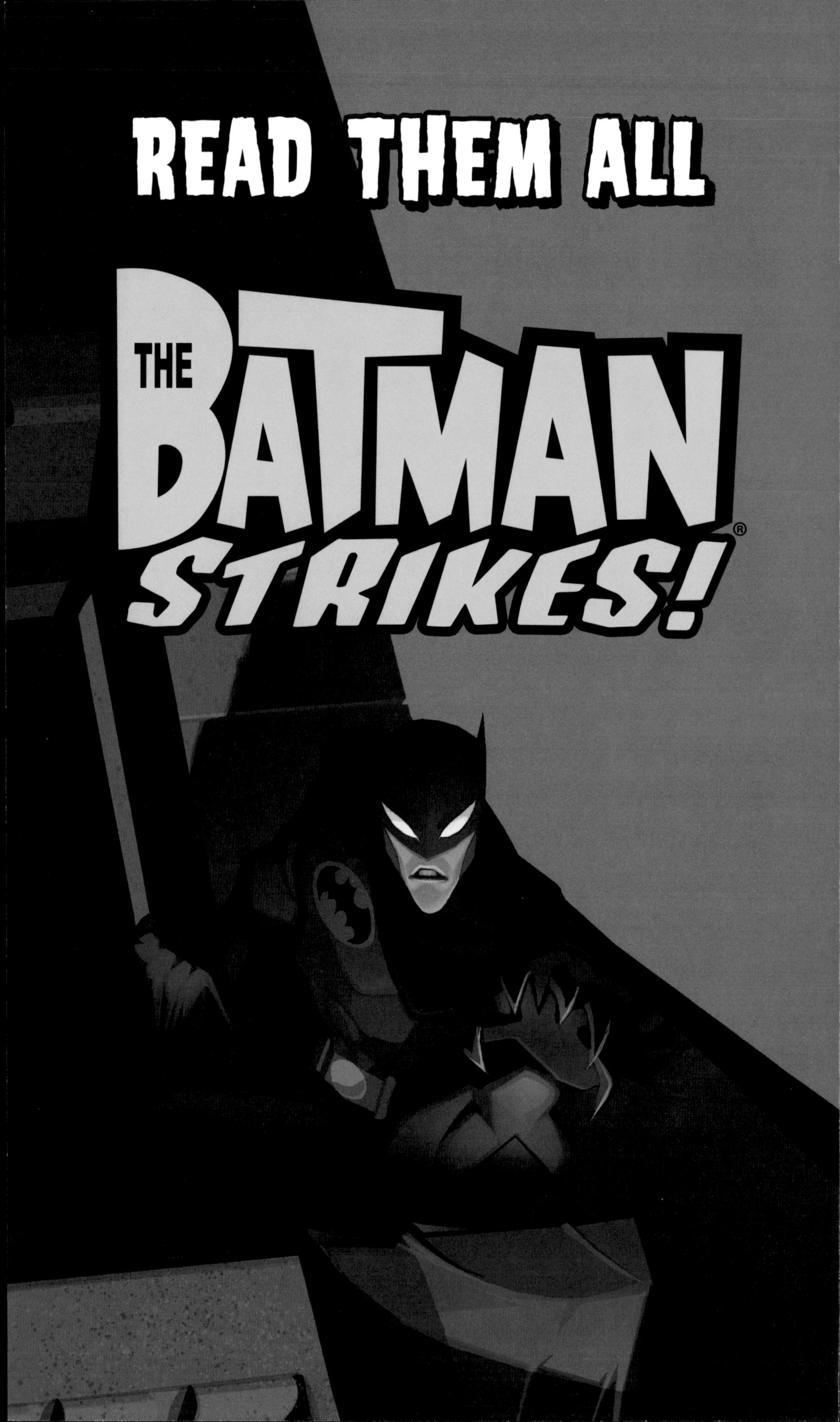
READ THEM ALL
THE BATMAN STRIKES!®

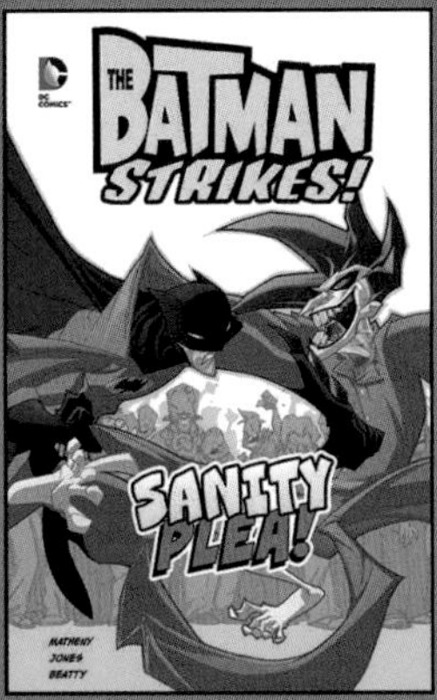
THE BATMAN STRIKES!
SANITY PLEA!
MATHENY
JONES
BEATTY

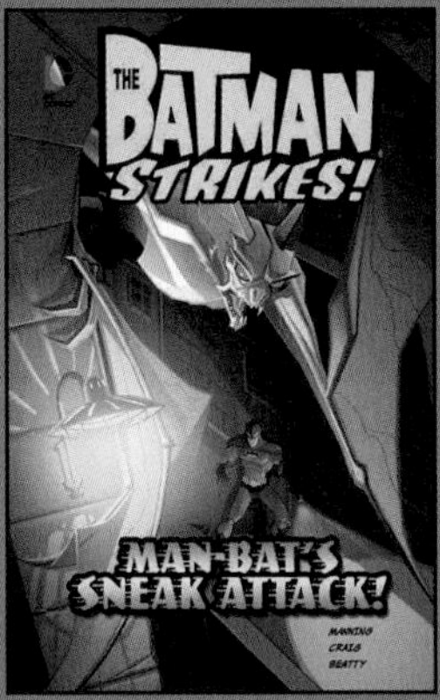
THE BATMAN STRIKES!
MAN-BAT'S SNEAK ATTACK!
MANNING
CRAIG
BEATTY

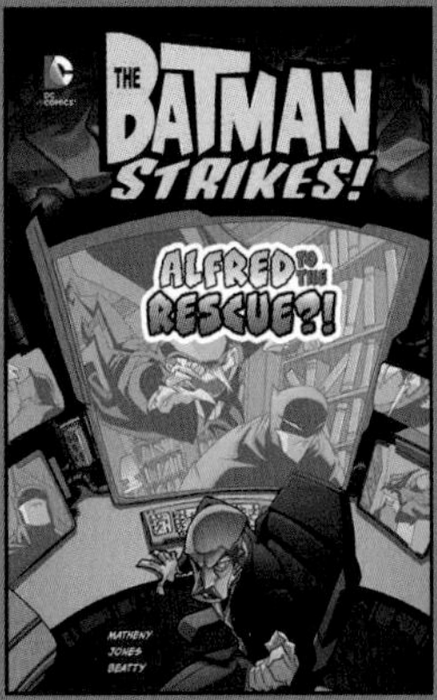
THE BATMAN STRIKES!
ALFRED TO THE RESCUE?!
MATHENY
JONES
BEATTY

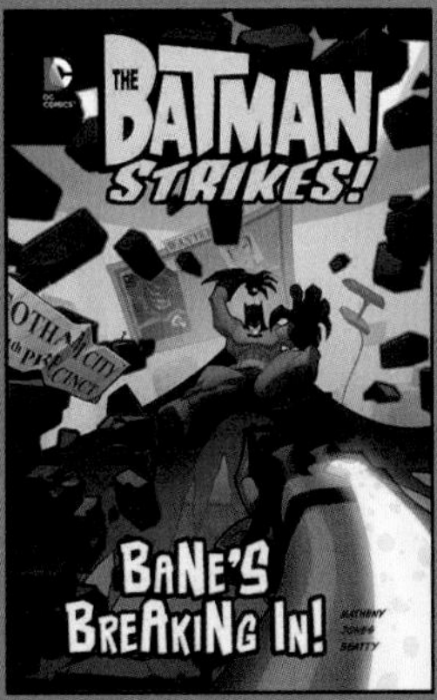
THE BATMAN STRIKES!
BANE'S BREAKING IN!
MATHENY
JONES
BEATTY

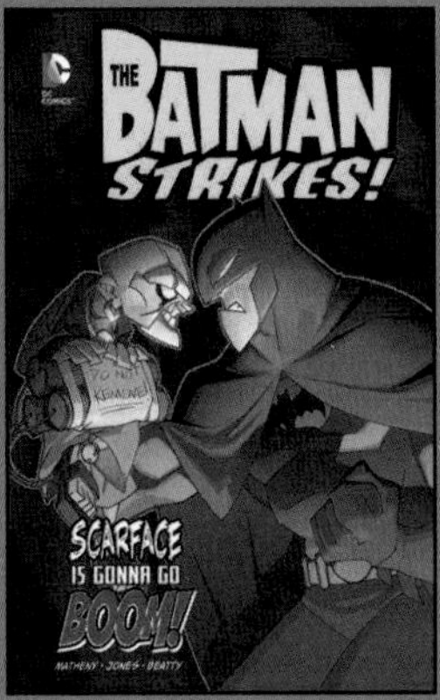
THE BATMAN STRIKES!
SCARFACE IS GONNA GO BOOM!
MATHENY · JONES · BEATTY

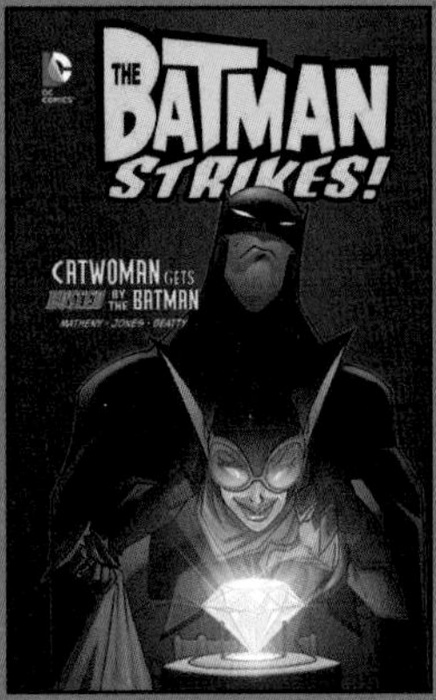
THE BATMAN STRIKES!
CATWOMAN GETS BITTEN BY THE BATMAN
MATHENY · JONES · BEATTY

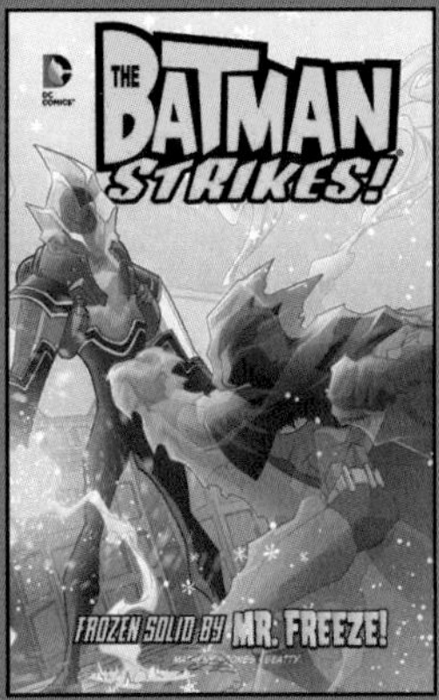
THE BATMAN STRIKES!
FROZEN SOLID BY MR. FREEZE!
MATHENY · JONES · BEATTY

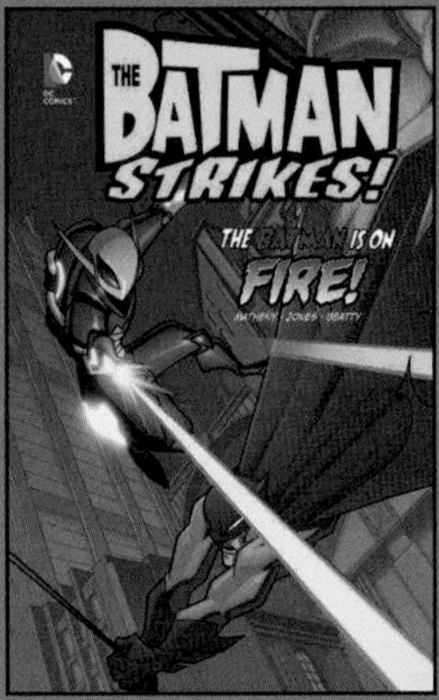
THE BATMAN STRIKES!
THE BATMAN IS ON FIRE!
MATHENY · JONES · BEATTY

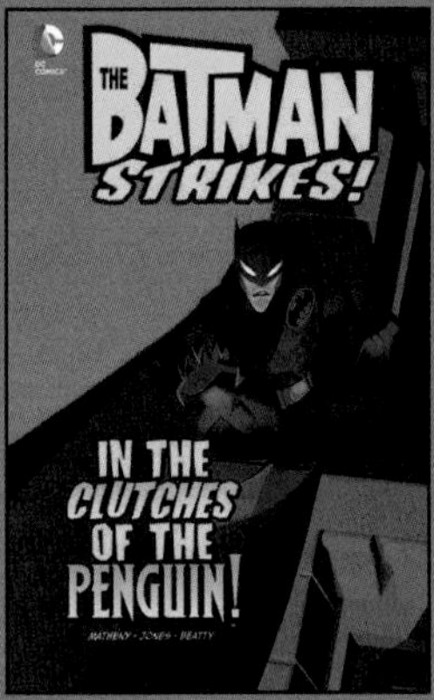
THE BATMAN STRIKES!
IN THE CLUTCHES OF THE PENGUIN!
MATHENY · JONES · BEATTY

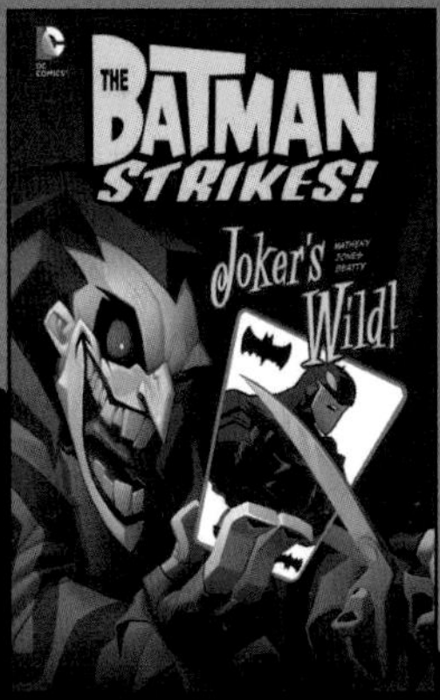
THE BATMAN STRIKES!
Joker's Wild!
MATHENY
JONES
BEATTY

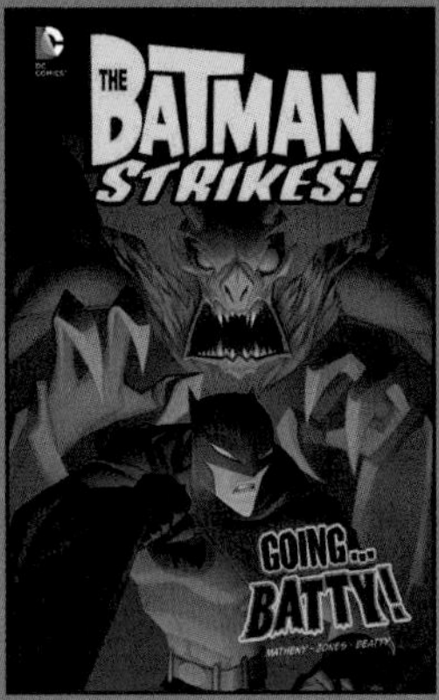
THE BATMAN STRIKES!
GOING... BATTY!
MATHENY · JONES · BEATTY

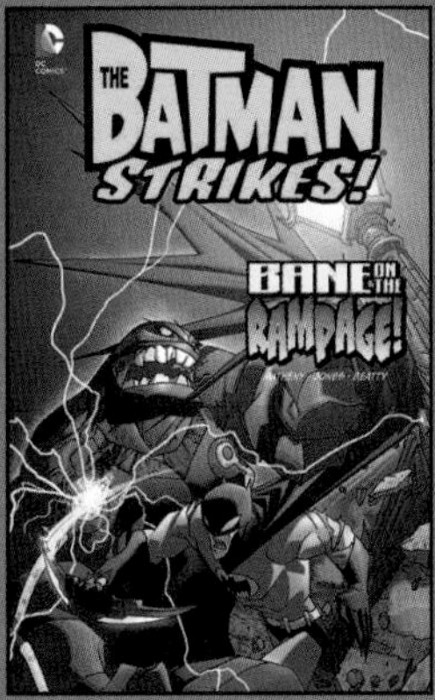
THE BATMAN STRIKES!
BANE ON THE RAMPAGE!
MATHENY · JONES · BEATTY

THE BATMAN® STRIKES!

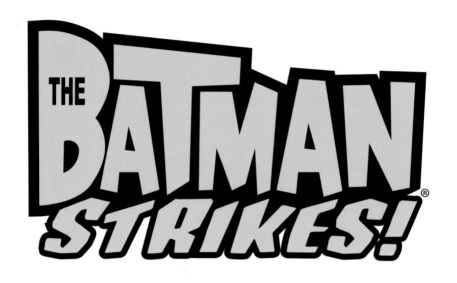